W9-BDH-242

DATE DUE

FEB 0 2 2009

DISCARD

DEMCO 128-5046

DISCARD

Mount Tamalpais School

Presented to
Mount Tamalpais
School Library
in honor of

Susan Butcher

by

Kate
for Tekla

Bad Dog School

Bad Dog School

by **Barbara M. Joosse**

Illustrated by **Jennifer Plecas**

CLARION BOOKS • New York

Mount Tamalpais School

Clarion Books
a Houghton Mifflin Company imprint
215 Park Avenue South, New York, NY 10003
Text copyright © 2004 by Barbara M. Joosse
Illustrations copyright © 2004 by Jennifer Plecas

The illustrations were executed in watercolors.
The text was set in 17-point Zemke Hand ITC.

All rights reserved.

For information about permission to reproduce selections from this book,
write to Permissions, Houghton Mifflin Company,
215 Park Avenue South, New York, NY 10003.

www.houghtonmifflinbooks.com

Manufactured in China

Library of Congress Cataloging-in-Publication Data
Joosse, Barbara M.
Bad dog school / by Barbara Joosse ; illustrated by Jennifer Plecas.
p. cm.
Summary: Harris's family decides that his dog Zippy should go to dog
obedience school, but after he is trained, they miss the old Zippy.
ISBN 0-618-13331-3
[1. Dogs—Training—Fiction. 2. Dogs—Fiction. 3. Pets—Fiction.]
I. Plecas, Jennifer, ill. II. Title.
PZ7.J7435Bad 2004
[E]—dc22   2003017173

ISBN-13: 978-0-618-13331-4
ISBN-10: 0-618-13331-3

SCP 10 9 8 7 6 5 4 3 2 1

For Patricia McConnell—
friend and teacher to Anneke.
Thank you.
—B.M.J.

To Marianne, Edward,
and Charlie,
with thanks.
—J.P.

Zippy was like a shook-up pop bottle—ready to explode. And that's the way Harris liked him.

Pirates was their favorite game. They sailed the open seas and searched for treasure. When they found some, Zippy buried it. Sometimes, they got dirty . . .

. . . and Mom sent them to the tub to clean up. The bath was the perfect place for a water battle. Harris made waves in the water, *blop, blop,* while Zippy blasted their enemies. *Kabloosh!*

Afterward, Harris dried off with a fluffy towel.

Zippy dried off with toilet paper.

When it was time for bed, Harris made a tent out of his blanket. He and Zippy crawled underneath. Harris shined a flashlight into his mouth to turn it red, and Zippy power-licked his face. "You're my best friend," said Harris. "You make everything more fun."

But Mom, Dad, and Eileen thought Zippy was getting into too much trouble. One day, things got a lot worse. Harris made the whistle sound: *Woo, wooooooo*. Zippy made one even louder. *AaaaaaaooOOOOOO!*

Eileen was trying to talk on the phone. "Cut it *out*, Zippy!" she yelled.

"AaaaaaaaooooooooooO!"

Zippy howled.

Eileen stomped into Harris's room. "Bad dog!" she yelled.

Zippy's tail drooped. "We were just having fun," Harris said.

When it was time to fix dinner,
Dad reached for the pork chops,
but they weren't there.

They were on the floor.
Zippy was tasting them.
"Bad dog!" Dad said.

Zippy hung his head and slunk away.

Then he buried his bone . . .
in Mom's herb garden.
Eileen discovered the disaster.
"Bad dog!"

Zippy scurried into the living room with his tail between his legs.

There was Harris on the soft, white sofa. Zippy jumped up for a cuddle.

"EEEEEEEK!" screamed Mom.

At dinner, everyone ate canned ravioli instead of pork chops. "Something has got to be done about that dog," Mom said.

"Zippy doesn't mean to be bad," said Harris. "He's just a little . . . zippy."

Dad was diplomatic. "Zippy *is* enthusiastic," he said. "But he's also out of control."

14

Zippy snarfed a ravioli off Eileen's plate. "No kidding," said Eileen. "He needs to go to obedience school."

"What's that?" asked Harris.

"It's a school for bad dogs," Eileen said. "Like Zippy."

That night, Harris cuddled Zippy under the blanket-tent. "I don't think you're a bad dog," he said. "But I don't want everyone to be mad at you. Maybe we'd better give obedience school a try."

Zippy slurped Harris on the cheek.

18

The next day, they went. At first, things didn't go very well. Zippy dug for buried treasure in the dahlias.

Then he made the whistle sound. "AaaaaaaaooOOOOOO!" All the other dogs went crazy.

The head teacher, Mrs. Pride, wiped a drizzle of sweat from her forehead. "We'll start with the basic commands," she said.

"Sit!" Harris said.
Zippy ran around
in circles.

"Stay!" Harris said.
Zippy power-licked his face.

20

Zippy and Harris practiced the commands . . .

. . . until Zippy got the idea.

At last, Zippy was obedient and well groomed. At graduation, Mrs. Pride presented her star student. Harris yelled, "Yahoo!" and opened his arms for a tumble and a big juicy dog kiss.

But Zippy licked his hand delicately, and that was all.

At home, Harris said, "Let's dig for treasure!"
But Zippy watched politely. "What's the
matter, Zippy?" Harris asked.

Mom ate popcorn and let a piece accidentally drop on the floor. Zippy licked his doggy lips but didn't eat it. "Zippy?" Mom asked.

Eileen snuggled on the sofa and reached for Zippy. But Zippy had been trained to stay off the furniture. She had to hug her stuffed bunny instead.

24

Zippy sat alone in his dog basket. He was clean and well behaved. He even smelled like dog perfume.

"Zippy certainly is polite," said Mom.
"And fancy," said Eileen.
"Yeah, but he's no fun!" said Harris.

Everyone agreed. They wanted the fun Zippy back . . .
but with some manners. Harris curled up with Zippy in
the dog basket while the rest of the family negotiated.

"I don't care if he eats people food," said Mom,
"as long as he doesn't swipe it off the table."

"And maybe he could be on the sofa," suggested Eileen,
"as long as he's not a dirtball."

"How are we going to get the fun Zippy back?" asked Dad.

"I know," said Harris. "We can retrain him at BAD DOG SCHOOL!"

Everyone thought Harris's plan was brilliant.
They got right to work.

Soon everything was ready for Bad Dog School.
It was time to call the star student. Harris gave
the command. "Come, Zippy." He stood in the
herb garden and said, "No digging."

Then Harris took Zippy to the special garden
he and Dad had fixed. It was full of bones!
"Dig," he said. But Zippy didn't dig.

Dad was the one to show him how.
"Like this!" he said, digging on his hands
and knees . . . until Zippy got the idea.

When Zippy went inside, Harris stopped him
with a command. "Sit," he said, and Eileen
wiped Zippy's muddy feet.

Zippy trotted into the living room. Mom
covered the sofa with a sheet. Harris gave
the command, "ZIPPY, COME!"

Zippy perked up his ears and bounded up!